WINDOW MUSIC

For Grandpa Maurice, Mom and Dad, and my husband Cliff . . . train lovers all. —A. S.
Thank you, Dad, for all you were, and thank you, Mom, for all you are. —W. Z.

VIKING
Published by the Penguin Group
Penguin Putnam Inc., 375 Hudson Street, New York, New York 10014, U.S.A.
Penguin Books Ltd, Registered Offices: Harmondsworth, Middlesex, England

First published in 1998 by Viking, a member of Penguin Putnam Books for Young Readers

1 3 5 7 9 10 8 6 4 2

Text copyright © Anastasia Suen, 1998   Illustrations copyright © Wade Zahares, 1998
All rights reserved

LIBRARY OF CONGRESS CATALOGING-IN-PUBLICATION DATA
Suen, Anastasia.
Window music / by Anastasia Suen ; illustrated by Wade Zahares.   p. cm.
Summary: Describes the trip taken by a train as it travels over hills,
through valleys, past horses and orange trees until it arrives at the final station.
ISBN 0-670-87287-3
[1. Railroads—Trains—Fiction. 2. Stories in rhyme.] I. Zahares, Wade, ill. II. Title.
PZ8.3.S9354Wi 1998 [E]—dc21 97-27306 CIP AC

Printed in Hong Kong   Set in OptiFob

WINDOW MUSIC

by Anastasia Suen
illustrated by Wade Zahares

Viking

train on the track
clickety clack

behind the sign,
cars in line

street after street
under our feet

wooo! wooo!
passing through

along the way,
horses play

in a row,
oranges grow

clickety clack
train on the track

**waves splash,
breakers crash**

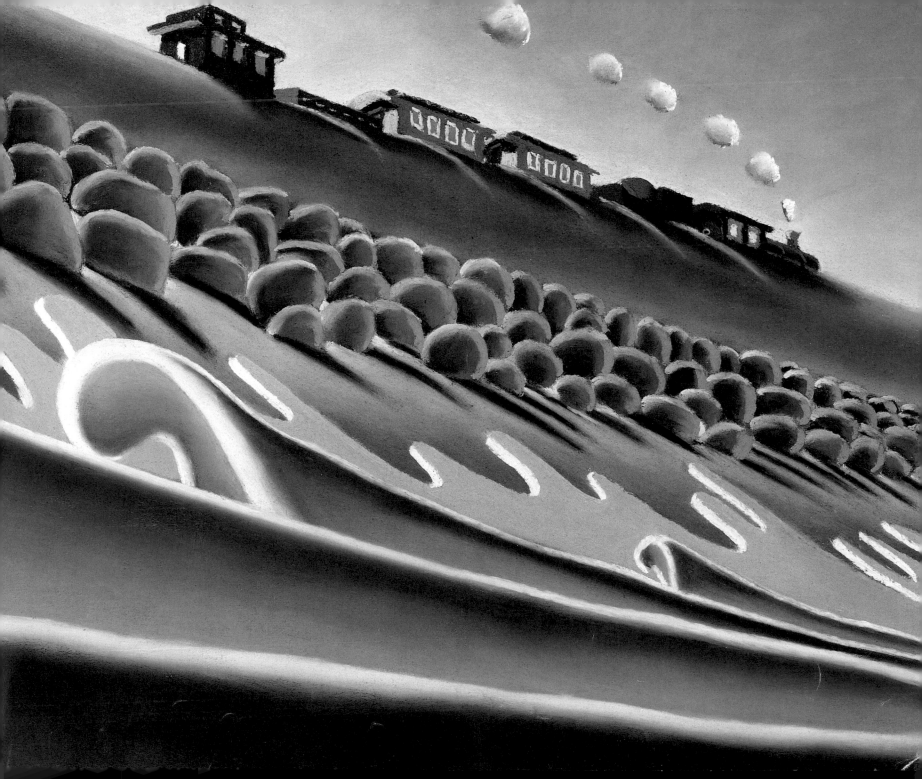

banana trees
sway in the breeze

over a hill,
grapevines spill

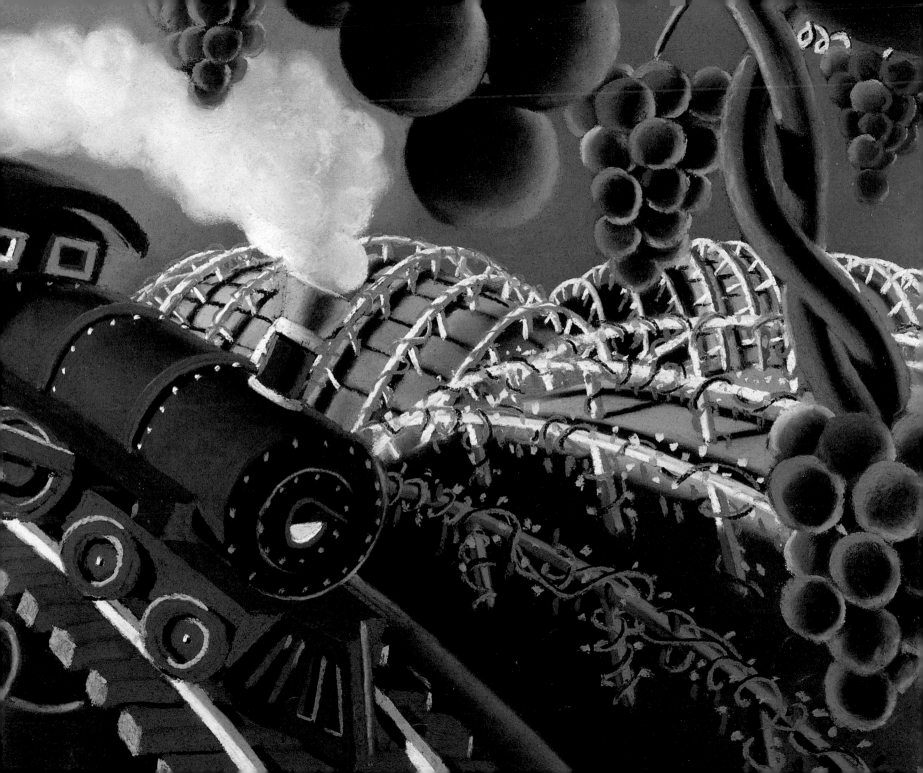

so high,
touch the sky

valley below,
down we go!

houses, streets,
the city repeats

into the station,
our destination

train on the track
clickety clack